Good Night, D.W.

by Marc Brown

LITTLE, BROWN AND COMPANY

New York ❧ An AOL Time Warner Company

It was time for bed.
Dad tucked in D.W. and gave her a kiss. Mom turned on the nightlight.
She gave D.W. a kiss, too.
"Good night, D.W.!" they said together.

D.W. tried to fall asleep. But she couldn't. She was wide awake.
"Is anybody out there?" she called.

Arthur came in. "What's the matter?" he asked.
"I can't sleep," said D.W.
"When I can't sleep, I think about one of the Bionic Bunny's adventures," said Arthur. "That always tires me out."

"I bet the Bionic Bunny has trouble falling asleep," said D.W.
"He must have a lot on his mind, too."
Arthur rolled his eyes. "Good night, D.W.!" he said.
"I've got homework to do."

"Is anybody out there?" D.W. called again.
Dad came in. "What's the matter?" he asked.

"I can't sleep," said D.W.

"Try counting sheep," said Dad. "Nice, fluffy sheep jumping over a fence."

"Did you ever wonder about sheep?" said D.W. "When do they sleep? They must not have time if they're so busy jumping over fences."

Dad sighed. "Good night, D.W.!" he said. "See you in the morning."

"Is anybody out there?" D.W. called a third time.

Mom came in. "What's the matter?" she asked.

"I can't sleep," said D.W.

"Just relax," said Mom. "Think about happy things . . . like going to the beach."

"But whenever I go to the beach, my bathing suit gets full of sand. I could never sleep thinking about all that itchy sand on me."

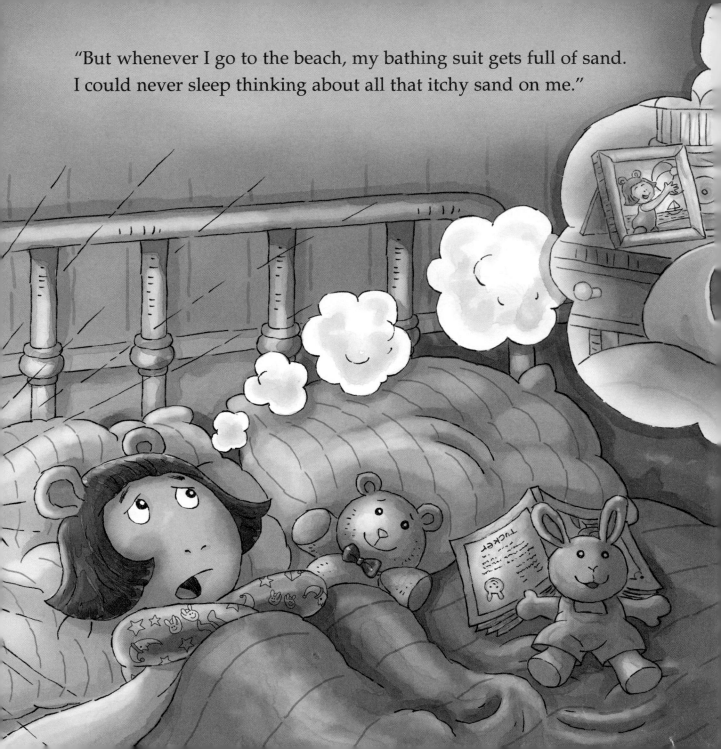

Her mother shook her head. "Good night, D.W.!"
she said. "Close your eyes."

D.W. closed her eyes. She tried thinking about the Bionic Bunny.

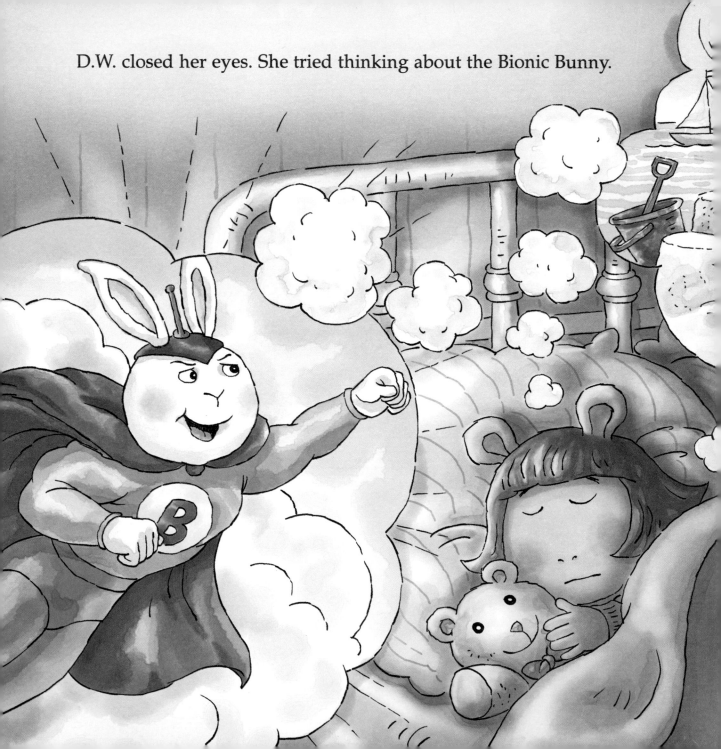

And the beach.

And fluffy white sheep.

But of course, none of it worked.

This time everyone rushed in together.
"What is it now?" asked Dad.

"How do you expect me to sleep?" said D.W. "The wind is blowing. And the bed is creaking. And Kate is making weird sounds!"
D.W. stopped to blink a few times.

"Besides, a tree could fall on the house. And there could be
a monster under the bed. Or in the closet. Or both!"
D.W. yawned a giant yawn.

"There are a gazillion reasons why I can't fall asleep," said D.W., closing her eyes. "I could go on . . . and on . . . and on . . ."
And she did.

But only in her dreams.

Good night, D.W.!

Dear Santa,
This is my Christmas list. It's short.

"What I Want for Christmas," from Ava
1. On Christmas Eve, I want to meet you.
Love,
your friend Ava

Dear Ava,
Santa is very busy, so he asked me to write and tell you that he received your Christmas list.
Merry Christmas!
Mrs. Claus

Dear Ava,

Wow. Those are a bunch of questions. I'll answer them in order:

1. People dress up like me to spread holiday cheer. I like having their help.

2. I can't explain to you how I get through the chimney and why I don't get burned in fireplaces. I'm not certain how it works, but it sure is fun.

3. I have other ways of delivering presents to homes that don't have chimneys. For security reasons, I need to keep that information secret.

4. No, I can't make it snow. That's Mother Nature's job.

5. Since you live in the north, you just might have a "white Christmas." But lots of children can never have a white Christmas because they live in hot places, like Hawaii or Mexico. It's still Christmas there, just a warm Christmas with no snow.

Merry Christmas!
Santa

P.S. Remember to send me your Christmas list.

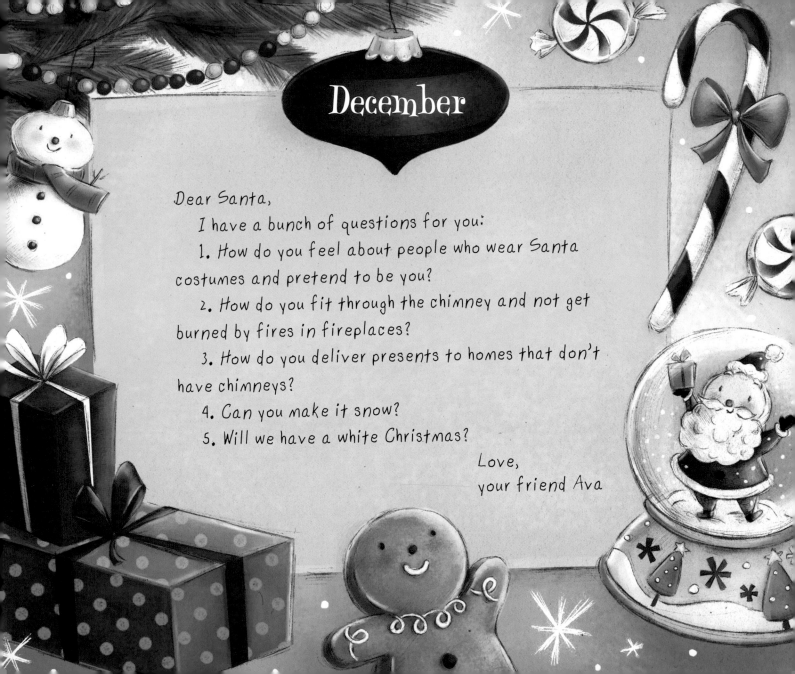

December

Dear Santa,

I have a bunch of questions for you:

1. How do you feel about people who wear Santa costumes and pretend to be you?

2. How do you fit through the chimney and not get burned by fires in fireplaces?

3. How do you deliver presents to homes that don't have chimneys?

4. Can you make it snow?

5. Will we have a white Christmas?

Love,
your friend Ava

November

Dear Santa,

Happy almost-Thanksgiving! People at school are talking about their Christmas lists, and some of the kids are saying you're not real. A couple of boys called me a baby for believing in you and said Christmas presents come from our parents. Is that true?

Love,
your friend Ava

Dear Ava,

I'm real to the people who believe in me—like you. But the holiday season is a time for everyone to give gifts, and I'm grateful for that. If I were the only person giving presents, I'd need a much, much bigger sleigh.

Merry Christmas
(and happy Thanksgiving)!
Santa

Dear Ava,

   We're too busy to celebrate Halloween. We are working day and night to get ready for Christmas. I'm sending you a bow and gift tag to wear with your costume, and the elves are including one of their hats for Corinne. You'll both look great! Mrs. Claus has enclosed two candy canes for your trick-or-treat bags.

   Happy Halloween and . . .

Merry Christmas!
Santa

October

Dear Santa,

Do you celebrate Halloween in the North Pole? I'm going to dress up as a Christmas present, and my cousin Corinne is going to be an elf.

Love,
your friend Ava

Dear Ava,
I actually don't celebrate my birthday—just Christmas! As for my age, all I can say is I'm much older than you, and your parents, and your grandparents, and your great-grandparents, and your great-great-grandparents. . . .
Merry Christmas
(and happy birthday)!
Santa

September

Dear Santa,

   I'm in first grade now and just turned seven.
I had red and green decorations on my birthday
cake. We played pin-the-tail-on-the-reindeer.
When's your birthday? How old are you?

                                    Love,
                                    your friend Ava

Dear Ava,

I love to swim! The reindeer, elves and I go swimming when there are breaks in the ice. We're sometimes joined by friendly seals, walruses and polar bears. And yes, I do go to the beach. Mrs. Claus and I take a summer vacation before our busy Christmas work begins.

Merry Christmas!
Santa

Dear Ava,

   We don't have fireworks here, but I can see the fireworks that are set off in Alaska and Maine. Also, since the sky in the North Pole is very dark at night, and the stars are so twinkly and bright, it's like seeing fireworks—especially when there's a shooting star! Happy Fourth of July and . . .

   Merry Christmas!
   Santa

July

Dear Santa,
   Happy Fourth of July! Can you
see the fireworks all the way up in
the North Pole? I bet your fireworks
are red, white and green.
   Love,
   your friend Ava

Dear Ava,

No, your brother did not contact me. Remember, he doesn't believe in me. So no, you are not on my Naughty List. It's been a very long time since I've had to leave coal in anyone's stocking, and I'm glad for that. I get very dirty when I have to carry coal.

Merry Christmas!
Santa

June

Dear Santa,
    My brother says he's telling you to put coal in my stocking because I went into his room when he told me to "keep out!" I was in there to look for our cat. Have you put me on the Naughty List? Please don't give me coal for Christmas.

                                    Love,
                                    your friend Ava

Dear Ava,

We do plant flowers and gardens in the North Pole! We plant special Christmas flowers. They're called poinsettias. Mrs. Claus and the elves care for them in our greenhouse. They also tend the vegetable garden, where we grow the corn that helps my reindeer fly.

Merry Christmas!
Santa

Dear Santa,
 The red tulip bulbs my mom and I planted are blooming. We're also growing green beans from seeds. Do you plant flowers and gardens in the North Pole?
 Love,
 your friend Ava

Dear Ava,

No, I haven't met the Easter Bunny. He and I work during different times of the year. As for what your brother said, your mother is right. Don't let him make you feel bad. Some people, like you, believe in me—and in the Tooth Fairy and the Easter Bunny—and some people, like your brother, don't. That's okay. So happy Easter and . . .

Merry Christmas!
Santa

April

Dear Santa,

That's so cool you met the Tooth Fairy. Have you met the Easter Bunny too? I told my brother your story but he says the Tooth Fairy isn't real—<u>and he says you're not real!</u> He also told me the Easter Bunny isn't real. My mother says he's just teasing me because I'm younger than he is. She says I shouldn't let him get me upset.

Love,
your friend Ava

March

Dear Santa,
 I lost a tooth last night. The Tooth Fairy came but I didn't see her. Do you know the Tooth Fairy? Here's a picture of me without my tooth.

Love,
your friend Ava

Dear Ava,

 I have met the Tooth Fairy. We bumped into each other one Christmas Eve when I was delivering presents and she was collecting a little boy's tooth. Since we both work late at night, after everyone is asleep, we accidentally frightened one another. The Tooth Fairy pulled out her wand—like she was going to zap me! When we realized who the other was, we started laughing. Turns out, the Tooth Fairy uses her wand like a flashlight. It can't zap anyone.

Merry Christmas!
Santa

P.S. That's a nice photograph of you missing a tooth. Thank you for sending it.

Dear Santa,
   Happy Valentine's Day! Since you're trying to eat fewer sweets, I drew this picture of you and your elves instead of giving you candy. Why did you end your letter by saying Merry Christmas? It's not Christmastime.
                    Love,
                    your friend Ava

February

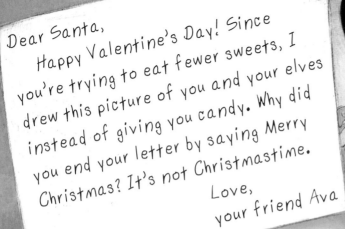

Bee Mine

Dear Ava,
   Thank you for the great drawing. People usually don't think of me on Valentine's Day. Well, Mrs. Claus does, of course, and I think of her. I love giving gifts, but it's also nice to receive them. I say Merry Christmas all year long, so . . .

                    Merry Christmas!
                    Santa

Dear Ava,

   Thank you SO much for your letter. Children usually write to me <u>before</u> Christmas. It was great to receive a letter after Christmas, and I'm glad you liked your presents. In answer to your questions: I always have room in my belly for cookies, but I'm trying to eat fewer sweets. Next Christmas, instead of cookies, maybe you can leave me some carrots. My reindeer love carrots, and it's good for me to eat vegetables. Yes, I know that you are six years old and are in kindergarten. Other things I know about you: You're a super-fast runner—like my reindeer—and you are working toward your black belt in karate. I have a black belt myself. Really, look at a picture of me. <u>Ho, ho, ho!</u>

Merry Christmas!
Santa

P.S. I go to bed early on New Year's Eve. I'm tired from all my Christmas work.

January

Soon after Christmas,
Ava wrote a thank-you note to Santa Claus.

Dear Santa,
    Thank you for my Christmas presents. I really like them.
But why didn't you eat the cookies I left you? Were you full
from the cookies at our neighbors' houses? I'm six years old
and I go to kindergarten, or did you already know that?
                            Love,
                            your friend Ava

P.S. Happy New Year! What do you do in the North Pole on
New Year's Eve?

My Pen Pal, Santa

Random House New York

By Melissa Stanton ⭐ Illustrated by Jennifer A. Bell

For Brian, Jack, Corinne and, of course, Ava

—M.S.

For my mom, Lil

—J.A.B.

Text copyright © 2013 by Melissa Stanton
Cover and interior illustrations copyright © 2013 by Jennifer A. Bell
All rights reserved. Published in the United States by Random House Children's Books,
a division of Random House, Inc., New York.
Random House and the colophon are registered trademarks of Random House, Inc.
Visit us on the Web! randomhouse.com/kids
Educators and librarians, for a variety of teaching tools, visit us at RHTeachersLibrarians.com
Library of Congress Cataloging-in-Publication Data
Stanton, Melissa.
My pen pal, Santa / by Melissa Stanton ; illustrated by Jennifer A. Bell.
pages cm. — 1st ed.
Summary: "When Ava writes a thank you to Santa in January, he writes back and sets off a year's worth of correspondence
where they exchange information about their daily lives and discuss their shared love of Christmas." — Provided by publisher.
ISBN 978-0-375-86992-1 (trade) — ISBN 978-0-375-96992-8 (lib. bdg.) — ISBN 978-0-375-98625-3 (ebook)
1. Santa Claus—Juvenile fiction. [1. Santa Claus—Fiction. 2. Christmas—Fiction. 3. Pen pals—Fiction. 4. Letters—Fiction.]
I. Bell, Jennifer (Jennifer A.), illustrator. II. Title.
PZ7.S79333 My 2013   [E]—dc23   2012042911
MANUFACTURED IN MALAYSIA
10 9 8 7 6 5 4 3 2 1
First Edition
Random House Children's Books supports the First Amendment and celebrates the right to read.